ROBOT REBELLION

Don't Miss Any of Astrid's
Out-of-This-World Adventures!

The Astronomically Grand Plan

The Unlucky Launch

Hydroponic Hijinks

Robot Rebellion

ASTRID THE ASTRONAUT

ROBOT REBELLION

By Rie Neal ★ Illustrated by Talitha Shipman

ALADDIN

New York London Toronto Sydney New Delhi

ALADDIN • An imprint of Simon & Schuster Children's Publishing Division • 1230 Avenue of the Americas, New York, New York 10020 • First Aladdin hardcover edition February 2023 • Text copyright © 2023 by Rie Neal • Illustrations copyright © 2023 by Talitha Shipman • Also available in an Aladdin paperback edition. • All rights reserved, including the right of reproduction in whole or in part in any form. • ALADDIN and related logo are registered trademarks of Simon & Schuster, Inc. • For information about special discounts for bulk purchases, please contact Simon & Schuster Special Sales at 1-866-506-1949 or business@simonandschuster.com. • The Simon & Schuster Speakers Bureau can bring authors to your live event. For more information or to book an event contact the Simon & Schuster Speakers Bureau at 1-866-248-3049 or visit our website at www.simonspeakers.com. • Book designed by Laura Lyn DiSiena • The illustrations for this book were rendered digitally. • The text of this book was set in Ionic No 5. • Manufactured in the United States of America 0123 FFG • 2 4 6 8 10 9 7 5 3 1 • Library of Congress Control Number 2022942030 • ISBN 9781534481572 (hc) • ISBN 9781534481565 (pbk) • ISBN 9781534481589 (ebook)

FOR CHRISTY, MY SISTER
AND FRIEND
—R. N.

TO MY DAD, FOR ALL THE
LOVE AND SUPPORT YOU GIVE
—T. S.

CONTENTS

ROBOT REBELLION

★ CHAPTER 1 ★

A VISITOR AT NIGHT

"Which episode was your favorite?" I asked my best friend, Hallie. I smoothed out my sleeping bag in front of the TV in the living room.

She put a finger to her chin. "Hmm . . . the one where the kitten cadets played jump rope. They were in zero gravity. The rope got all tangled!"

Hallie tossed her pillow onto a pile of blankets. She didn't like sleeping bags. For sleepovers she just burrowed into blankets like a bunny.

I grinned. "And then they bumped the controls. The spaceship was heading for a black hole!"

"And AstroCat had to untangle them. Before they all got sucked in!"

"But then Tabby-Droid saw that it was really just a blob of Rolfo's blackberry jam on the screen. It wasn't a black hole at all!"

We burst into giggles. Season five of *AstroCat* had dropped a week ago. We'd each watched it once already. Now we were going to watch it together.

I thought about Tabby-Droid. He could walk, talk, and fly a spaceship. In Shooting

Stars, the after-school space-themed club I was in, we were about to start a new Astro Mission. Ms. Ruiz had said we'd be coding a *real* robot. Tabby-Droid was a robot. Would it act like him?

I grabbed my TV necklace—a small box attached to a loop. It worked with my hearing aids to help me hear the TV better. Next to me, Hallie snuggled into her blankets. Using the remote, I turned on the show.

Mom poked her head in. "You girls all set?"

We nodded.

"I'm heading to bed. Lights out by ten, okay?"

"Okay, Mom."

"Okay, Mrs. Peterson."

Mom headed down the hall to her and Dad's room. My big sister, Stella, was in the room we shared, probably texting her friends.

3 ⭐

Since I had a friend over, we got to sleep in the living room.

AstroCat's theme song started up. Slipping my TV necklace around my neck, I pressed the button on the box. But the song still sounded fuzzy, so I tried again. The theme song burst into the best part: "*. . . AaaastroCat can save the day! She can always lead the way!. . .*" The box still wasn't working, but I knew the song.

Hallie was singing along. Then I heard, "AAAAAAAAH!" She jumped up onto the couch.

I paused the show. "What's wrong?"

Hallie pointed down the dark hallway. "You didn't get a pet, did you?"

I scrambled up beside her. "N-n-noooo."

Down the hall, something was creeping toward us. The whole condo was dark, except for the TV. It cast weird shadows as the thing got to the living room.

"It's coming closer!" Hallie hissed. "What if it's a rat? Our neighbor has them. They have red beady eyes and—"

"It's not moving like a rat." I squinted at it.

The thing passed through a bit of light from a window.

"But it's furry like a rat!" Hallie whispered. "We should tell your parents."

"We'd have to go past it to get to them."

The thing stopped. Tiny red eyes blinked at the wall. Then it turned toward the kitchen.

"See?" Hallie whispered. "Rats go for food."

But something was off about this "rat."

I stepped off the couch.

"Astrid!" Hallie grabbed my arm. "What are you doing?"

But I shook her off. I put a finger to my lips. The thing was in the kitchen now, around the corner of the wall. There were bumping noises, and then nothing. I tiptoed closer. And closer. And—

The thing spun around to face me. A claw-like hand gripped a pack of chips. "Want a snack?" it asked.

"Aaaaaaaaaaaaaa!" I vaulted back to the

couch as Hallie and I both screamed.

Laughter bubbled out from the hall. My sister lowered her phone. "That was the *best*! I wish I'd had better light for the video."

My cheeks heated. "Stella! That was so not cool."

"You scared us!" Hallie said.

Stella made herself stop laughing. "I'm sorry. Just . . . Do you know how long it took to write the code to get him to do that?"

I frowned, flicking on the lights. I stooped to pull off a furry brown hat with eyeholes. Under it was a blue-and-white robot. It had two treads for feet and two claw-arms. Plus a small screen on its tummy.

"What is it?" Hallie asked.

"It's the newest Code-a-Bot." Stella beamed.

"He's called 'Cory.' He's a super high-tech, ultra-expensive robot. I borrowed him from our robotics club."

"Hey!" I said. "That's what we're going to use on Monday!" I'd never seen a Cory before. He didn't look as fancy as Tabby-Droid. But he could still do a lot.

"I'm sorry I scared you guys," said Stella. "Pretty good, though, huh?"

Stella didn't look that sorry. But it *was* pretty cool. Not a lot of people had a robot who could get them a snack.

I tugged at the chips in Cory's claw, but he wouldn't let go.

Stella helped me rip the bag free. Chips spilled onto the carpet.

She frowned. "Well, *that* still needs work." She bent to clean up. "See, I have to create the perfect routine for Cory. I got into the regional Code-a-Bot competition. It's in two weeks. There will be a *lot* of people there." She bit her lip.

"Maybe don't have him surprise them in the dark, and you'll be good," Hallie said, back in her blanket mound. "We thought he was a rat."

Stella giggled. "Sorry."

"Hey, can you fix my TV necklace? It's not working." I handed it to her. Stella always fixed my stuff. If it had buttons, Stella could fix it.

"Sure!" Stella set down her phone. She fiddled with the box I wore, then checked its dock on the TV. She reached back where all the cables were. "All fixed. There was a cable loose."

She handed the necklace back to me. Hallie hit play on the remote. *AstroCat* sounded like *AstroCat* now.

"Thanks!" I said.

"And thanks for the chips," Hallie added.

Stella shrugged. "That's what big sisters are for."

CHAPTER 2

MS. RUIZ HAS A SECRET

"I heard Cory can do backflips," said Veejay.

Ella leaned in. "And spins."

"And cartwheels," Veejay added.

Dominic had the biggest smile of all. "I heard he can do your homework for you."

I raised an eyebrow. After meeting a Cory, I wasn't sure that last one was true.

The cage for the STEM lab's new bunny

sat under a window near our table. Pearl had named him Galaxia the Super Space Bunny. We'd started calling him "Gal" for short. Pearl made kissing noises at him.

Ms. Ruiz raised her hands for quiet. As kids found their seats, she clipped my hearing aid mic to her shirt. "Okay." Her voice now sounded like she was right in front of me. "Today's the day." She grinned, then pointed to a shiny blue-and-white robot on the lab table behind her. "You guys all know these Code-a-Bots are not cheap. Thanks to a generous donor, Shooting Stars is able to have our own Cory."

Ella nudged me and whispered something.

"What?" I asked.

She pointed to the back of the room. "Pearl's mom and dad," she whispered louder. "She has one of her own at home too."

Back in her seat across the room, Pearl tossed her ponytail.

Oh brother.

"As I've told you all," continued Ms. Ruiz. "Coding a routine for Cory is your next Astro Mission. But since we're new at this, there won't be a competition. You'll each get three points for the Astro Board just for working hard for the next three weeks. If anyone wants to share their Cory routine then, we'd love to see it. But sharing isn't required to get the points."

I frowned. I mean, that was nice, but . . . I'd really wanted our group to have the *best* routine.

"Let's watch a quick demo video first." Ms. Ruiz pressed a button on a remote, and the lab's TV sprang to life. The Cory on-screen danced to music. He did cartwheels. He played fetch. He pointed to walls of different colors and said "blue" or "black" or "yellow."

"Wow," breathed Veejay.

The video kept going. Cory waved hello back to a boy. He gave a girl a thumbs-up about her homework.

Dominic nodded smugly. Ella rolled her eyes at him.

Finally, Cory popped a wheelie. He waved and then rolled backward, out of the shot.

Wow, I thought. *Maybe Cory is a lot like Tabby-Droid!*

A speaker came on next, but she sounded too fuzzy. Ms. Ruiz had forgotten to put my clip-on mic next to the TV! I was about to raise my hand when I heard something.

". . . isn't a big deal."

Ms. Ruiz must've still been wearing the mic. I glanced around the room, trying to see where she had gone. I finally spotted her at the back of the room, by the door. She was talking with another teacher. One I didn't know.

"It's the twenty-fifth, right? We should have a party," said the woman.

Ms. Ruiz wrinkled her nose. "I don't want to make a fuss. Shooting Stars has plenty going on, and so do my STEM classes."

"You're turning *thirty*," the teacher said. "You have to do *something*."

I blinked. Ms. Ruiz had a birthday coming up?

"I'm too busy right now. I'll celebrate later. Don't worry."

"Suit yourself." The teacher patted Ms. Ruiz's shoulder. "I just want you to feel taken care of."

Ms. Ruiz smiled. "Thank you."

But as the teacher walked away, Ms. Ruiz looked sad for a second.

I whipped back around to face the front. I mean, I felt bad about listening in, but I couldn't really help it. She was the one who'd left the mic on.

But . . . I couldn't believe Ms. Ruiz hadn't told us about her birthday.

I didn't even try to listen to the rest of the video. My foot bounced up and down. I couldn't wait to tell the others. Finally, the credits rolled.

Veejay raised an eyebrow at me. "You're shaking the table."

"I just heard something," I whispered back. "About Ms. Ruiz."

Ms. Ruiz strode back to the front and clicked off the video.

Veejay and I snapped our mouths shut.

"Pretty cool, right?" Ms. Ruiz said. "But Cory doesn't do fancy tricks on his own. *You* have to figure out the code to make it happen. Your first routines will be *very* simple. You'll work in groups of four, on class laptops. Save the code to these Cory sticks." She shook a baggie of purple data sticks. "And then you'll be able to plug them into Cory to test your code. There is a guide on each table."

Ella looked at me, Veejay, and Dominic. "Group?"

"Obviously," said Dominic.

I leaned in, almost bursting now. "Guys! I heard Ms. Ruiz say that her birthday was coming up. She's turning thirty, and she's not celebrating!"

Veejay frowned. "How do you know that?"

"She was wearing my mic during the video. I heard her talking with another teacher."

Ella's eyes got big. "Everybody should get to celebrate their birthday. If they want to."

"Maybe she doesn't want to," said Veejay.

I shook my head. "She told the other teacher she was too busy—helping *us*. We have to do something."

"But what?" asked Ella.

Dominic scratched his chin. "We could buy her a pony."

Ella scowled at him. "We can't afford a pony."

"We could bake her a cake," said Veejay. "But I'm not allowed to use the oven."

Around us groups were getting to work. They were getting laptops off the cart. They were reading the guides. Up front, Ms. Ruiz was showing Pearl and Noa how to get Cory to spin in a circle.

I thought back to the weekend and how Cory had held out chips to us.

That was it!

"I know what we can do!" I told my friends. "We can code the best routine ever for Cory. And at the end, he can give her flowers and a card. That can be our present to Ms. Ruiz!"

"That's perfect!" said Ella. "We need a routine anyway, and that will show her how much we love her!"

"*And* it will be fun." Veejay grinned.

"I still think we should go with the pony," said Dominic. "Who doesn't love ponies?"

We all raised our eyebrows at him.

"Okay, okay," he said. "Geesh. A Cory routine sounds great."

"A *perfect* Cory routine," I said. "With flowers and a card."

"But didn't she say the coding was hard?" asked Ella. "What if we can't get Cory to do what we want?"

My mouth curved upward. "Oh, don't worry about that," I said. "I have a secret weapon when it comes to Cory." I reached for the guide. "Leave it all to me."

★ CHAPTER 3 ★

HELP? OR NOT . . .

"Stella?" I raced through the front door, tossing my backpack in the hall.

The video we'd watched today had made it look super easy to make Cory do things. But after we started working, all our group had gotten done was getting him to roll forward and backward. *That* didn't look very cool.

But I knew we could do it. We just had to get Stella's help. She'd been working on a Cory for *months*. She was a pro.

"Slow down, Astrogirl," Mom said. "Where does your bag go?"

"Sorry." I picked up my backpack and set it on the bench by the door.

"We're ordering from Ramen Hut. What would you like?"

"Again?" Ramen was great and all, but so was *pizza*.

Mom shrugged. "I know. But it's Stella's favorite, and she has a lot of work tonight. You might not want to bother her."

"She's my sister." I rolled my eyes. "And I need her help." I scurried down the hall and burst into our bedroom. "Hey St—"

Stella sat on the floor by her bed. Her laptop

was in front of her, and she was frowning at the screen.

"Hey, sis." I stepped around her and bounced onto my bed.

"I can't talk right now, Astrid." She started typing.

I spotted a purple data stick plugged into her laptop. "Hey!" I pointed. "That's for Cory, right?"

She squinted harder at the screen. I crossed the room to sit on *her* bed, so I could see it.

I blinked. Her code was a *lot* more complicated than what we were learning.

"Yes. I'm working on my routine for the competition." Stella hit the run button. She'd had to return her club's Cory this morning. But the little Cory on screen showed what the routine would look like with a real Cory. It was called the simulator. We'd used it in

Shooting Stars earlier today too.

The Cory on-screen zigzagged in between some cones. It did a dance. It put its arms up and stomped its feet. It spun in a circle. It did a cartwheel—or tried to. The little Cory toppled over, and Stella groaned.

"I'm never going to get this in time!"

I patted her shoulder. "Sure you will." I was about to tell her our plan and ask for her help, but she moaned.

"We just got the list of requirements," she said. "I still need to add a lot. And we have to be up onstage to present our routine. I really don't like getting up in front of people. Also, I found out the worst news ever—*Mr. Baines* is going to be one of the judges!"

"Who?"

"He works at our school. He's, like, the

grumpiest teacher ever. He's going to be awful as a judge!"

"I'm sorry, Stella. That sounds bad."

"It is! And I *really* want to win. The top five people go to the state championship!"

"Wow." I shrugged. "But it'll be okay. You're great at this stuff."

"No, I'm not, Astrid. I *love* this stuff. But . . . it's a lot of work. I'm going to be up to my ears in code, 24/7 until the competition!"

I flopped back on her bed—24/7?

Stella was upset. She was probably exaggerating. Stella was always there when I needed her. She was my big sister.

After she got her own stuff ready, I could ask her for help with mine. Knowing Stella, she'd be done in a day or two—maybe even later tonight. I'd just have to wait.

★ CHAPTER 4 ★

SISTER TROUBLE

The rest of the week went by. I kept waiting for Stella to be in a better mood, but she never was.

Maybe I just needed to put the problem right in front of her. Then she wouldn't be able to *not* help. Just like with my TV necklace. Or my math homework. Or the five thousand other things Stella helped me with. We could still build our perfect Cory routine for Ms. Ruiz.

So Saturday morning I had my friends over. Veejay hunched over my laptop at the coffee table. Ella sat next to him. She flipped through the Cory guide. Dominic was hanging upside down on one of the armchairs.

We'd been at it for half an hour. But Stella still hadn't come out of our room yet, so she hadn't seen us. Plus, she had friends of her own over. I hadn't expected that.

"Astrid, do you have pastels?" Hallie called from the kitchen. She and Chantal had come over too. As soon as I'd said we needed a card for Ms. Ruiz, they'd said they would help.

"What are pastels?" I asked.

Hallie sighed. "Never mind."

Ella pointed to the screen. "Look, there's

an error in your code. It's like this." She shoved the guide in front of Veejay.

He jerked his head back to keep from getting hit in the face. "Hey!"

Dad set a plate of cookies on the table. "I'll be in my office. Your mom is in the kitchen if you need anything."

I picked up the list of moves we'd written down. There were nineteen things on it. The routine ended with Cory rolling to where one of us would be and taking the flowers and card. Then he would roll over and hand them to Ms. Ruiz. Finally, he'd sing her the happy birthday

song. Ms. Ruiz would smile so big. She'd hug us and say she'd never had such great students before.

I frowned at the screen. "I thought we were going to have him do a little dance first."

Ella scowled at me. "This *is* our dance."

Veejay groaned. "We need help, guys. Or we need to wait till Ms. Ruiz teaches us more." He pointed at the list. "There's no way we're going to figure out all those moves on our own."

"But the whole point is to surprise her," I said. "If we ask her for help, she'll know what we're doing."

"Okay, so, what about that secret weapon, Astrid?" Ella folded her arms across her chest. Veejay and Dominic waited.

I nodded. "Right. I'll . . . go get it."

Maybe it was a good sign Stella had friends

over. Maybe it meant she was done with her code. And then she could help us. Stella would fix everything.

I pushed our bedroom door open. It was now or never. "Stella?"

The room was quiet. Stella and her two friends were all staring at their screens, typing. One of her friends was sitting on *my bed*. A dirty backpack spilled open next to her. She'd scattered my pillows, and AstroCat was on the floor.

"That's my bed," I said.

"Oh. Sorry, kid." The girl stuck her feet out so they weren't on the bedspread anymore. She'd had her shoes on my bed too?!

"Stella," I said through clenched teeth.

Her eyes were still fixed on her laptop screen. "Hmm?"

"Can your friend please sit on *your* bed?"

But Stella ignored me. She tapped some keys, then groaned.

"Did you calibrate at the start?" asked her other friend. Crumbs fell onto the floor as he bit into a cookie.

"Yeah. It's something else."

"Maybe he's not lifting his arm high enough."

I raised an eyebrow. "Are you guys working on Cory routines?"

"Of course we are," Stella huffed. "Regionals are in one week! Can you close the door, please?"

"And we need more cookies." The kid on the floor held up a crumb-filled plate.

My cheeks burned. Stella's friends were being rude, and Stella didn't care. Not only

that, but she seemed even busier than before. And my friends and I *needed* her help.

I got right in front of Stella. "When are you going to be done? I need to ask you something."

Stella's eyes got super big. She pointed to her laptop, then at the door. "Oh my gosh, Astrid. We have *one week* left. Please!"

I slammed the door behind me. In the hallway, I took a deep breath, trying not to cry. I'd been kicked out of my own room. Stella wouldn't even listen to me. I no longer had a secret weapon. Did I even have a sister?

★ CHAPTER 5 ★

A NOT-SO-PERFECT ROUTINE

"Dominic got Cory to talk," Ella said.

It was Monday after school, and we were in Shooting Stars. Ms. Ruiz was going from table to table, helping kids with their code.

I blinked. "That's great!" We'd need to know how to do that before we could make him sing. We'd finally decided we needed a shorter routine. We'd spent the rest of our time on

★ 38

Saturday on the card. Hallie and Chantal had done a great job. They'd decorated it with bits of code they'd gotten from the Cory guide. We'd all signed it. The card was perfect.

Now we just needed the routine to go with it. And we weren't much closer on that.

"How did he figure it out?" I asked.

"He watched Ms. Ruiz. She was showing another group how to do it."

I frowned. "Oh. I hope he didn't spoil the surprise."

"I don't think he did." Ella grimaced. "We still don't know how to make him *sing*, though. We really need that secret weapon."

"I know. It's . . . not ready yet."

I hadn't talked to Stella since Saturday. When she was home she was in our room. She made me feel like I couldn't even go in there. At least Mom and Dad had said they'd talk with Stella about her friends sitting on my bed.

"We need to cut more stuff," Veejay said.

"We've already cut like ten things!" I wailed. "If we cut any more, Cory will just be rolling forward and backward and saying 'happy birthday.'" I'd tried to read the guide by myself on Sunday. But it was filled with words I didn't know. Words like "operator" and "variable."

"Hey, when are we going to have Cory do the routine for her?" asked Dominic. "If we wait till the end of the Astro Mission, it'll be too late."

"Hmm," Ella said. "Well, her birthday is this Saturday. But we don't see her on weekends."

Ms. Ruiz appeared at our table. "And how are *these* Shooting Stars doing?"

We jumped. Had she heard us talking about her birthday?

"Uh . . ." I swallowed. "Fine."

She put her hands on her hips. "Can I see what you've got so far?"

Ella glanced at me. "It's . . . We need more time."

"No worries! You have plenty of time. And no one's going to see this except me."

That was the problem.

Ms. Ruiz moved closer to see our laptop screen.

But Ella had just typed the words "happy birthday" into our code.

I slammed the laptop closed.

Dominic jumped. "Hey!"

Ella nudged him to be quiet.

Ms. Ruiz frowned. "Is everything all right?"

"We're just fine, Ms. Ruiz. Thanks!" Ella put on a fake smile. The rest of us copied her. We nodded so hard, I'm sure we looked like bobble-head dolls. "No help needed here!"

"Well . . . okay." Ms. Ruiz stepped back. "Let me know if you need anything."

Once Ms. Ruiz had moved on, Ella groaned. "She totally suspects."

"I know," I said. "I feel like we're letting her down."

Veejay shrugged. "Don't worry. When she sees our routine, she'll understand."

I hoped Veejay was right.

The bell rang then.

"Oh no!" said Dominic. "We didn't get much done."

Ella left to take the laptop back to the cart.

"Hold up," Ms. Ruiz called to everyone from

the door. "This Saturday is the regional competition for Cory coding. I'll be helping out. And some former Shooting Stars will be competing. Since you're all working with Cory too, I thought you might like to see the action. If you do, I'll see you there. Give this flyer to your parents." She handed out papers to kids as they left.

"My sister's going to be in it," I told my friends. "I'll be there anyway."

Veejay's eyes lit up. "Sounds like fun."

Ella ran back, waving a flyer at us. "Guys! This is on Ms. Ruiz's birthday! You know what that means?" Her eyes bugged. "We can do the Cory routine there!"

Pearl was nearby, filling the bunny's water. "Ms. Ruiz has a birthday this Saturday?"

I nodded, then turned back to Ella. "You have to be really good to get into regionals, Ella. We're not even close."

"No, no, no," she said. "I don't mean we *enter*. I mean, there will be a Cory there. We could bring our data stick and the card and flowers. Cory could do the birthday routine at the end—just for her."

"Wait." Pearl leaned over, sticking up a hand. "You're doing a special routine for Ms. Ruiz?"

I bit my lip. Pearl hadn't always been the nicest person to me. "*Please* don't tell her, Pearl."

She smirked. "Fine. But I want in. Plus, my aunt is going to be a judge at this thing. I'll talk to her about using the Cory. If it's for Ms. Ruiz, I'm sure she'll say yes. They go way back."

I blinked.

"Great!" said Dominic.

"Ms. Ruiz helped us figure out a spin," Pearl said. "You can add it to your routine if we get to sign the card. Can you guys handle adding it?" She raised an eyebrow. It was a challenge.

"Of course we can!" Ella shot back. "Besides, Astrid has a secret weapon."

I swallowed. "But . . . will that be okay with your group?"

"Obviously." Pearl's ponytail swished as she ran off.

"This is perfect!" said Veejay. But then he frowned. "Except . . . if we're doing the routine Saturday, we need to finish it by Friday. We still have a ton left to do." He bit his lip. "Will your secret weapon be ready by then, Astrid?"

"What *is* the secret, Astrid?" Ella folded her arms across her chest. "I think you should tell us now."

They stared at me, waiting.

And yes. This *was* great. But what if I couldn't get Stella to help? Really, they were all counting on *me*. I'd told them I'd take care of it.

I swallowed. "Well . . . if I told you, it wouldn't be a secret."

Ella groaned. "Astr—"

"But will it be ready by Friday?" Veejay asked.

"Uh . . . yeah. Absolutely."

My stomach didn't feel so good. Everybody was going to see this routine now—not just Ms. Ruiz. The whole club would see it. And their parents. Maybe other people too.

Was this how Stella felt? Our routine wasn't even in the competition. No mean judge would be yelling at us. And there was no state championship to worry about.

For the first time, I felt bad for not thinking about how *she* felt. I should have tried to understand her better.

As we left, I slipped the guide into my backpack. Somehow, I had to make this mess right—both for Stella and for my friends.

★ CHAPTER 6 ★

HELP IS A FUNNY THING

That night, I beat Stella home.

I went straight to our bedroom. Except for sleeping, I hadn't been in here much lately. And tonight I had work to do. I needed quiet. So I took my hearing aids out and sat on my bed with the Cory guide.

But as I was opening it, I looked around our room.

Stella's side of the room was a *mess*.

It always made *me* feel better when my stuff was neat. Maybe she felt that way too.

So I got up. I made her bed. I scooped building bricks into an empty box and shoved them underneath. I put her clothes into her hamper.

I was just hanging a sweater up in the closet when I felt a breeze—the door had opened.

Stella came in like a storm. But when she saw her bed, she stopped. "Mmr oo—"

I held up a hand for her to wait. I put my hearing aids back in. After the start-up jingle, I faced her. "Okay, what?"

"Did you make my bed? And clean up my stuff?"

I shrugged.

She let her backpack slide to the floor. I

watched as it landed in a sad-looking heap.

"Astrid, I'm sorry. I haven't been very nice lately."

I took a deep breath. "I know you're worried about the competition."

But Stella just flopped onto her bed. "Mmmfmhm hmmpf," she said into her pillow.

"What?"

She rolled over. "I'm quitting. I'm not doing it."

"Why not? You love robots!"

"Yeah, I do." She sniffed. "But it's too much. Mr. Baines yelled at me just for going too fast in the halls today. I can't stand in front of him as a judge. And I can't get the cartwheel. That robot just does what he wants to. The cartwheel alone would earn me enough points to have a shot at winning. Without it, I'm out."

My mouth hung open. Stella could fix

anything. My sister *never* gave up.

I scrambled up to sit next to her. "Stella, I know you can do it. You're so good at coding. You made Cory come in and give us a snack, remember?"

Stella sat up, hugging her knees. "I just . . . What if I freeze when I'm up there?"

"I'll be close by. You can look at me, and you'll feel better."

Stella's mouth twitched. "I think you've turned into the big sister." She frowned. "Hey— what did you want to talk to me about? You know, last Saturday."

I couldn't ask her anymore. I wouldn't.

"Oh . . . n-nothing."

Stella raised an eyebrow, and I hugged her. "I just want to help *you* right now," I said.

My friends needed me. But my sister did too.

☆ ☆ ☆

The next morning Mom drove me to school.

I knew I had to be honest with my friends.
This was *not* going to be fun.

Groaning, I pressed my forehead to the car
window.

Mom glanced back. "You okay?"

I could at least tell my mom.

So I spilled it all. I told her about our Cory
routine for Ms. Ruiz and how we weren't ready.
I told her about Stella and how I didn't know
how to help her.

My mom nodded. "Help is a funny thing, kiddo. Your sister loves being there for you. It's who she is. And you know what? I'm willing to bet that Ms. Ruiz feels the same way."

I frowned, thinking. "She did seem sad when we told her we didn't need any help."

"You're already helping Stella, just by being there for her. And Ms. Ruiz? She likes teaching you guys. She's not going to care if your routine isn't perfect. The best way to show her you care about her is to use what *she* has helped you learn. Whatever that is."

I slung my backpack over my shoulder as we pulled up to school. Maybe Mom was right. But Ms. Ruiz hadn't helped us with Cory. We hadn't let her. Was it too late to show her what she *had* taught us?

CHAPTER 7

FIXING

Later that day, everyone was out on the blacktop, and recess was noisy. Ella had her hands on her hips. Veejay looked worried. Dominic watched a ball bounce past. Hallie squeezed my hand—I'd told her everything in class. I didn't know how to fix it all, but I knew I had to fess up about Stella.

"What did you want to tell us?" asked Veejay.

My shoulders sagged. "I—I don't have a secret weapon."

"I knew it!" Ella groaned. "Why did you lie to us?"

"It wasn't a lie!" I protested. "I mean, I didn't mean for it to be. My sister is really good at Cory stuff. I thought she'd be able to help us, and we'd have the perfect routine for Ms. Ruiz. My sister fixes things. But . . . she's too busy."

"Astrid!" Ella said.

"I'm really sorry. I shouldn't have promised until I asked her."

Pearl ran up then, with Noa and another girl. "Here's the code for our spin."

Ella took the data stick from her.

Hallie opened the card for Pearl and her friends to sign.

"That's so cool you got Cory to spin," said Veejay.

"We wouldn't have gotten it without Ms. Ruiz."

And then, suddenly, I had an idea. Ms. Ruiz hadn't helped us—we hadn't let her. But she had helped all the other groups.

I turned to my friends as soon as Pearl was gone. "I know how we can save the routine!"

☆ ☆ ☆

We spent the rest of the week talking to the other groups. Most had coded only one or two moves, like us. And all of them were excited to surprise Ms. Ruiz.

By Friday we had a paper bag full of purple Cory sticks. The next day was Ms. Ruiz's birthday, and we had a lot of work to do. My friends had come over to help.

We were just setting up when Stella walked in. "You guys are here again? What are you working on?" She pointed to the pile on the coffee table. "Are those Cory sticks?"

I bit my lip. Should I tell her? She still hadn't changed her mind about the competition. I was hoping I could talk her back into it later tonight. I didn't want her to be too stressed out until then.

But before I could decide, Dominic blurted out the whole thing.

Stella's eyes got big. "You're doing a birthday Cory routine for Ms. Ruiz? Why didn't you tell me?"

"I was going to. But I didn't want you to feel like you had to help," I said. "I know you've been stressed out."

"But we could still use help!" Ella said.

I shot her a glare.

"Well, maybe I could just take a look." And before I could protest, Stella had planted herself on the couch in front of my laptop.

We clustered around her. She scrolled through the code, making *hmm* noises. She paused. "Look," she said, pointing to a command. "You have the bracket on the wrong side."

Veejay smacked his forehead. "Ms. Ruiz talked about that. We should've caught it."

She plugged in one data stick after another. Her fingers flew as she added all our moves together. It was becoming a full routine! "And I'll give you the code I wrote for when I had Cory bring you snacks."

Ella said, "Isn't that cheating?"

Dominic rolled his eyes. "We aren't

competing. We're just doing this for Ms. Ruiz."

"Besides," Veejay said. "Stella used to be one of Ms. Ruiz's students. We'll say this is from her too."

Dominic stared at Stella's fingers as she typed. "Wow. You're really good at this stuff."

"Yeah," said Ella. "You're a lifesaver."

Stella blushed. "Oh. It's no big deal." She hit run. The Cory onscreen moved forward and backward first.

"That's our move!" Veejay pointed.

Then Cory went through the other groups' moves. Finally, he zoomed to one side to pick something up.

"That's when he gets the card and flowers from one of you," Stella said.

Then he zoomed back to where Ms. Ruiz would be. "Happy birthday," he said in a monotone voice.

We giggled and clapped.

"You're amazing," said Ella.

Stella laughed. "I'm not *that* great."

"Are you kidding?" Veejay said. "You just saved our routine. Ms. Ruiz will love it!"

Stella took our data stick out of the laptop. "These sticks all look alike. This is the one that has the whole routine on it. Don't get it mixed up with any others."

I tucked it into my pocket. "You almost got Cory to do a cartwheel, too," I said. "That's next level."

A sly grin spread over Stella's face. "Actually, I did figure it out." She took out a Cory stick with a flower sticker on it.

Our jaws dropped as she ran her routine for us. The Cory onscreen did figure eights around some cones. Then he stacked the cones one by one. He did a dance (better than just moving forward and backward). And at the end, he landed a cartwheel.

"That was amazing!" gushed Ella.

"Is that your routine for tomorrow?" Veejay asked. "You're going to win!"

Stella shifted. "Oh. Well . . ."

I grinned at Stella. Slowly, she smiled back. She took a deep breath. "I don't know if I'll *win,*" she said. "But I think . . . yeah. It *is* my routine for Saturday."

"Yes!" I leaned down to hug Stella.

My sister was competing. And we had an awesome birthday surprise for Ms. Ruiz—from *all* of us.

Nothing could go wrong now.

⋆ CHAPTER 8 ⋆

CORY COMPETITION

The auditorium was packed. The noise was so loud, I had to turn down my hearing aids. Veejay, Ella, Dominic, and I were in the front row. My mom and dad were there too. Around us, other Shooting Stars sat with their parents. Ms. Ruiz had stopped by to say hi, but then she had to go help out.

I patted my pocket, making sure our data

stick was still there. She was going to be so surprised!

Pearl tapped my shoulder. I couldn't hear what she said, but she passed me back the card. Other Shooting Stars had been signing it.

"Thanks!" I shouted.

Pearl smirked. She said something else and gave me a thumbs-up.

"What?" I yelled.

Next to me, Veejay said, *"Rrrr* aunt said *yeh.* About *yrrrrr* the Cory." My hearing aids couldn't get every word in the noise, but I could get enough of what he said.

Ella pointed to the flowers he held. They looked like half-dead weeds. "Those *oog* like you pulled them out of *yrrr* yard!"

Veejay ducked his chin. "I did," he said. *"Err rrr* all I could find."

"You *hrhrrr* supposed to buy *vmmm*," Ella said.

"*Rrrr* not that bad," Veejay groaned. "Right, Astrid?"

I made a face. At least we had the card. And

besides, the Cory routine was the real present.

Up on stage, a man cleared his throat. He and the rest of the judges were ready. They were all sitting behind a long table on one side of the stage. It was about to start!

"Maybe the flowers just need water," I told Veejay. "Give them to me. Stella said I could come backstage while she was doing her routine, and she's second. I'll stop by the bathroom after."

Dad and I scooted out of the row. He was coming backstage too.

We hurried to the nearest exit, then down a hall. It was nice to be away from the noise. I turned my hearing aids back up. Dad stopped at a door that had a sign that read STAGE. A high schooler wearing a headset opened it for us.

Backstage looked like a secret world. There

were ropes and pulleys and a million light switches. It smelled like sawdust and paint. But where was Stella?

Onstage, the man was still talking. He sounded pretty gruff.

"There you guys are!" Stella breathed. "I'm so nervous, I'm shaking. Look!"

Her hand jittered in the air.

I grabbed it. "You're going to do great, Stella. You've got this."

Dad rubbed her back. "Your mom and I are proud of you, Stella Bella. No matter what happens."

On the stage, the first kid was going on. We watched his Cory do a spin, then a somersault. But the grumpy judge yelled at him. The boy froze.

"That's Mr. Baines," Stella said, gripping

her data stick.

"What did he say to that boy?" Dad asked.

"He yelled at him for starting before he told him to."

"Yikes." Mr. Baines *was* grumpy.

We watched as the boy started over. After the routine the audience clapped. But Mr. Baines called the boy to come closer to the judges' table. It looked like Mr. Baines was doing most of the talking. The boy left with drooping shoulders.

"I can't do this," Stella said.

I grabbed her by the arms. "Yes, you can." I hugged her tightly, and something clattered to the floor.

"My data stick!" Stella shouted.

I scrambled after it. "Got it!"

Stella took the stick from me, but her eyes were on the stage. Her face was pale.

Another person with a headset leaned over. "Stella Peterson? It's your turn."

I squeezed her hand. Dad patted her shoulder.

The tech almost had to push her onstage. But finally, my big sister shuffled out to face the judges.

⋆ CHAPTER 9 ⋆

A REBELLIOUS ROBOT!

We watched Stella set up her cones. Her hands still shook a little. I tiptoed closer to watch, and my foot kicked something. It was a small, purple something.

I felt my pocket; it was empty! My data stick must've fallen out when I hugged Stella.

She was about to start. I grabbed the data stick off the floor and held it tight.

The Cory onstage started to move. He moved forward and backward.

Funny. I'd thought Stella's routine started off with the cones. Maybe she'd added this.

But when the Cory started a perfect spin next, I froze.

No.

All the sticks looked the same. I opened my hand, almost not wanting to look at the one I held. And sure enough, there was a flower sticker on it. We had switched!

I waved my arms at Stella, but she wasn't looking at me. She knew something was wrong. But just like she'd feared, she was too scared to move. She just watched in horror as Cory did the routine meant for Ms. Ruiz.

"Stella!" I hissed, holding up her data stick.

But she still didn't see me. And suddenly, Cory was rolling right at me.

I was still holding Ms. Ruiz's flowers. And I was standing right where I was supposed to be to hand them to him.

Cory's claw clamped down on the stems of the wilty flowers. He jerked them out of my grip.

And then I was frozen like Stella. Was this really happening?

Dad rushed up behind me. "What's he doing?"

Cory was doing what we'd programmed him to do. He rolled right up to where we'd planned to have Ms. Ruiz stand. But Ms. Ruiz wasn't onstage. Cory thrust the flowers out— to *Mr. Baines*—and wished him a happy birthday instead.

I slapped my forehead. Stella went pale.

But the audience thought it was hilarious. It started with a few giggles here and there. I peeked out to watch. But soon the audience was roaring so loud, I didn't need to see them to know they were laughing.

At Stella.

"Is this your idea of a joke, young lady?" Mr. Baines boomed. He stood up, towering over Stella.

Stella's eyes were huge. "N-n-no!"

I ran over, holding out Stella's data stick. "It's the wrong code!"

Now the audience's laughs turned into murmurs. And now everyone was staring at *me*.

But Stella was my sister. It was my turn to help her.

"And who are you?" asked one of the other judges.

"I'm Astrid, Stella's sister. We were both working on routines for Cory. Our sticks got switched." None of the judges were taking the stick from me, so I gave it to Stella.

We glanced back to Dad, but he wasn't there. Where had he gone?

I swallowed. The judges *had* to give Stella another chance!

"Please let her start over," I said to them. "She's been working so hard. It's my fault they got switched. I hugged her, and they both fell out. Then I gave her back the wrong one."

Still standing, Mr. Baines put his hands on his hips. But another judge hid a smile.

Mr. Baines sighed. "And are you in the competition, erm . . . Astrid?"

I shook my head. "We've been doing Cory routines in Shooting Stars. This one was . . ."

I stepped closer so I could whisper. "It was supposed to be a birthday surprise for Ms. Ruiz."

He glared at me and humphed.

Just then, Ms. Ruiz hurried out from the other side of the stage. Dad was right behind her.

Oh no! What if she'd seen the routine? The surprise would be ruined!

"Looks like I missed something." She looked between me, Stella, and the judges. "How can I help?"

"These girls are trying to cheat." Mr. Baines humphed.

Stella and I both shook our heads.

"No—" I said.

"Oh, sit down, John. Stop blustering," one of the other judges said to Mr. Baines. She nodded her short, gray curls at Stella. "You're scaring the poor thing to death." To Stella, she said, "It's all right, dear. Of course we will let you have a do-over."

Stella exhaled. "Oh, thank you!" She scurried off to get Cory ready again.

Mr. Baines shoved the mostly dead flowers at Ms. Ruiz. "I think these are for you. From Cory."

Ms. Ruiz's brow wrinkled as she took them. "Uh . . . thanks?" She motioned for my dad and me to go offstage with her.

Cheeks hot, I followed. I gave Stella a thumbs-up. At least she got to start over.

As soon as we were backstage again, Ms. Ruiz gave me an amused smile. "I have a feeling there's a story here, but I have to get back to the sign-in table."

But I had to ask. "Wait—Ms. Ruiz, d-did you see Cory's routine just now?"

She shook her head. "Your dad came running to get me. He thought maybe I could help. But no worries. I'll catch up with you after it's over, okay?"

As Ms. Ruiz left, my heart sped up. Maybe it wasn't too late after all!

CHAPTER 10

HAPPY BIRTHDAY

Several hours later, as the auditorium cleared out, Stella came running up to us.

"Fourth place!" She held up her medal. "I get to go to state!"

I met her halfway. "I knew you could do it! You're my hero, Stella."

She giggled. "No, you're *my* hero, Astrid.

How did you talk to the judges like that? I was so scared, I couldn't think!"

I shrugged. "Sisters take care of each other."

Stella smush-hugged me, and I smush-hugged back.

"Smile, girls!" Mom aimed her cell phone at us for a picture.

We grinned. "Cheese!"

Ella ran up. "Your routine was great, Stella!"

Veejay and Dominic and the others joined us.

"What about Ms. Ruiz?" asked Pearl. "We have to catch my aunt before they pack up the Cory!"

We raced backstage. I hoped we weren't too late.

"Where's your aunt, Pearl?" Dominic asked. "We don't know what she looks like."

"She's—" Pearl started.

"Pearl, dear. *There* you are." The judge with curly gray hair held out her arms. "Are you coming over for lunch tomorrow?"

I blinked. "*She's* your aunt?"

"I'm Aunt Rose," the woman told us. "Technically, *Great*-Aunt, but who's counting?" She waved a hand for us to follow her.

"She's also a science teacher," Pearl said. "At a middle school."

"She's the one who stood up for Stella!" I whispered to my friends.

"Cory is very tired." Aunt Rose winked at us. "But I think he has one more trick in him."

She led us over to Cory. His battery light was low. "Yes, indeed. Very tired. We'll need to be quick. What was it you wanted to do with him?"

"We have to find Ms. Ruiz," I said.

"I hope she didn't leave." Veejay scanned around us.

People were busy cleaning up. Someone put away the judges' table. Out in the audi-torium, most of our parents were helping to stack chairs. My mom and dad had come with us backstage, though.

I shook my head. "She said she'd see me after."

"Shooting Stars!" Ms. Ruiz came out from behind a curtain. She set down a box of papers. "So . . . what did you all think? Wasn't it great to see in person what Cory can do?"

We nodded, suddenly shy. Ella nudged me.

"We want to show you the routine we've been working on," I said. "It's . . . for you."

She blinked. "Okay."

Veejay scooted around to Cory's back. "Stick, please."

I handed it to him, and he plugged it into Cory's port.

Ella cleared the area. She pointed to one side. "Stand there, please," she told Ms. Ruiz.

Ms. Ruiz raised an eyebrow at my parents. They just shrugged, smiling, as if to say, *Wait and see*.

Ella stood a few feet away with the card behind her back.

I pressed the run button on Cory's touch-screen and backed up.

Cory moved forward and backward. Then he did a spin, and Pearl and Noa beamed. As he went through each group's move, those kids pointed and grinned. He did a cha-cha, then a somersault. He spun again.

Then he headed over . . . to me!

Ella and I were in the wrong places. She scurried over to shove the card into my hands. Cory reached out his claw. I stuffed the card into his claw-arm, hoping he wouldn't wrinkle the paper. Then he zoomed over to Ms. Ruiz. He handed her the card. And just as he squeaked out "happy birthday," his battery died.

Ms. Ruiz clutched the card to her chest. She had tears in her eyes. "How did you kids know it was my birthday?"

"Astr—" Dominic began.

"From another teacher," I cut him off. I

didn't want her to feel bad for leaving my mic on. "The flowers were for you, too. But then our data stick got switched with my sister's. Cory gave them to Mr. Baines instead."

"So *that's* what happened earlier!" Ms. Ruiz laughed.

"It's from everybody—we all put code in." I gestured to the whole group.

"We wanted you to know how much we like Shooting Stars," said Veejay.

"And to have a good birthday." Ella smiled.

"I thought we should get you a pony," said Dominic. "But I was overruled."

We rolled our eyes. But Ms. Ruiz gave a full-on belly laugh.

"Did you have an okay birthday?" I asked.

"Are you kidding? You guys made something with what I taught you. That's the best present ever!"

From the side, Mom winked at me.

We group-hugged Ms. Ruiz.

"Thanks for your help," I told Pearl's aunt Rose.

She had tears in her eyes too. "Teachers don't get thanked enough. I was happy to be a part of this. Now, you young, strong kids help me lift this dead Code-a-Bot back into his box. He needs to get home for a good charge."

Ella and I lifted Cory into his box.

"Sweet dreams," Dominic told him.

I said goodbye to everybody. Then my family walked out to the parking lot together. Stella couldn't stop staring at her medal.

"Well," Dad said. "Sounds like we need to go

out for dinner. We've got a fourth-place win-
ner and . . . an honorable mention, of sorts."

Stella and I giggled.

"Where do you want to go, Astrid?" she
asked.

Stella was always looking out for me. And
it was really nice. But I needed to look out for
her, too.

"Hmm . . . how about Ramen Hut?"

Stella's eyes lit up. She threw an arm
around my shoulders.

I grinned. "Sisters forever!"

AUTHOR'S NOTE

I'm an audiologist who supports access to language—whether it be spoken, signed, or both. I've written Astrid with hearing aids and spoken language because I'm the most familiar with that perspective, but I have great respect for the Deaf community and signed languages like American Sign Language (ASL). There are a lot of great books out there with deaf/hard-of-hearing characters that are written from other perspectives. For a starter list, find my profile on Instagram at @rienealwriter.

ACKNOWLEDGMENTS

First of all, thank you to YOU, Astrid's readers! I hope this book inspires you to reach for the stars.

As Astrid learns, things just don't work unless you find your team. I am very grateful to have the amazing Carrie Pestritto as my agent. It honestly would not have occurred to me to write an original chapter book series without her guidance. Thank you also to my wonderful editor, Alyson Heller, who saw exactly what I was trying to do with Astrid and loved her from the beginning—and to all the people at Aladdin and Simon & Schuster who made this book into a reality. I'm so honored to get to work with you all.

Many thanks to Danielle Kelsay, Diane Niebuhr, Stephanie Fleckenstein, and everyone else at the University of Iowa Au.D. program, for my education in audiology. Thank you to all the hospitals, clinics, schools, and other places that harbored me as an intern and to all the clients who inspired me along the way. (And special thanks to Amanda Baum, who helped a ton with drummer info for my last project and whom I wasn't able to thank properly then.)

I wouldn't have gotten this far without Leira K. Lewis, Victoria Kazarian, Rosanna Griffin, and Rebecca Cuadra George. Whispering Platypodes forever! Thank you also to SCBWI. And a million warm fuzzies to Teresa Richards, who brought me up to speed on publishing when I started writing and remains the best critique partner ever.

Finally, super big thanks to JMac and SL for putting up with their mom being sucked into pretend worlds all the time. Thank you to my parents for all their love and support. Thank you to Grammy & Pa, for all the visits to NASA Ames over the years. And thank you to Brian, who supported my writing from the beginning. I love you and would not be here without you. Finally, thank you to God for this opportunity.